George

Makes Friends

First published in the United Kingdom in 2005
by Chrysalis Children's Books,
an imprint of Chrysalis Books Group plc
The Chrysalis Building
Bramley Road
London W10 6SP
www.chrysalisbooks.co.uk

This book was created for Chrysalis Children's Books by Zuza Books.
Text and illustrations copyright © Zuza Books

Zuza Vrbova asserts her moral right to be
identified as the author of this work.
Tom Morgan-Jones asserts his moral right to be
identified as the illustrator of this work.

BRITISH LIBRARY CATALOGUING-IN-PUBLICATION DATA
A catalogue record for this book is available from the British Library.

ISBN 1 84458 482 8

Printed in China
2 4 6 8 10 9 7 5 3 1

George

Makes
Friends

Zuza Vrbova

Illustrated by Tom Morgan-Jones

CHRYSALIS CHILDREN'S BOOKS

George was always late home from school.
It wasn't that he was a slow walker. It was
just that George had an imaginary friend,
and there was a lot for George and his friend
to do. George's friend was called Gem.
He was George's best friend.

Nobody knew about Gem because nobody could see him except George. Gem was taller and stronger than George, and very good at games. Most importantly, he always said the right thing.

Every day, George met Gem by the big oak tree
in the playground at school. If George didn't have
anyone to play with, he talked to Gem.

And during lesson time, George liked to sit
at the back of the classroom. There was always
space there for Gem to sit next to him.

The good thing about Gem
was that George could tell him
anything. For example, how greedy
Fred was. Or how bossy Tabby was.
Or how George was planning to be
a dinosaur hunter when he grew up.

Gem always listened carefully and never made
a fuss. Then he would say, "As I was saying..."
and make a useful suggestion.

One day, George had a bad time at school.

Miss Roo asked him to spell HIPPOPOTAMUS.

George got stuck and stuttered halfway through.

Everyone laughed.

When he wanted to join in the skipping game,

Tabby said, "George, you always get tangled

in the rope. You're so clumsy. Go away!"

When he tried to join in the football game,

he let the ball into the net.

"George, you're so clumsy! Go away!"

Harry said.

So George did.

11

George plodded sadly towards the oak tree.

Gem was already there, waiting for him.

"As I was saying," he said,

"let's do something entirely different."

"But what?" asked George.

"We need a place of our own,"

Gem suggested.

"Yes, but how do we get one?"

asked George.

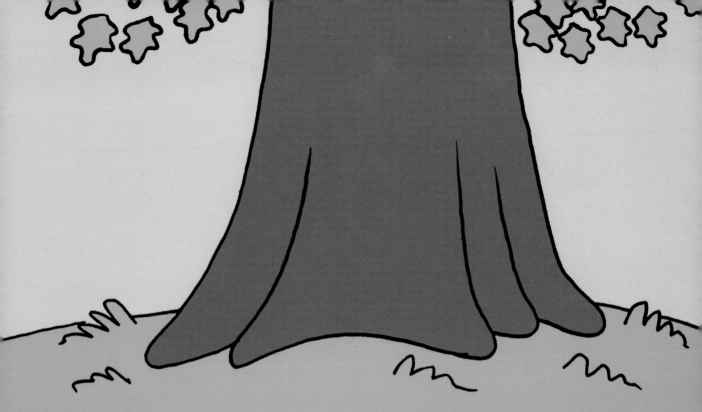

"Let's build a tree-house in the oak tree," said Gem.
He had his hands in his pockets and was leaning
against the oak tree, chewing on a twig.

So George went home and got all the things
he thought they might need. He got:

Biscuits (in case they got hungry)

His thick winter boots (in case it got cold)

His coin collection

A drawing he had done (to hang up)

His recorder (in case they wanted some music)

When George and Gem finished their tree-house,
they were very proud of it. It was beautiful.
It had walls made of glass and an arched wooden door.
A chandelier hung from the ceiling and a red carpet
covered the floor.

On the tablecloth, there were teacups and saucers
and a large teapot in the middle.

"As I was saying," said Gem, "why don't we have tea?"

They were just settling down when they heard a shout
from the bottom of the tree.

"Hey, what are you doing up there?"

It was Tabby.

"What shall we do?"

George whispered to Gem.

"Why not ask her up?" suggested Gem.

"But this is our private place!" said George.

"Yes," said Gem, "which means we can decide whether or not to invite other people to join us."

19

George began to think about this, but Tabby wasn't waiting

for an invitation. She was already halfway up the tree.

"What are you doing here, George?" she asked.

"Oh, it's just my tree-house," George answered,

trying to sound cool. "I was just tidying up a little.

It gets so cluttered sometimes."

"I didn't know you had a tree-house," Tabby said,

sounding impressed.

"What's all that?" Tabby asked, pointing at a sack
covered by leaves, pine cones and tree bark.

"That's the tea set. Would you like some tea?"
George lifted the largest pine cone, just as if it were a teapot.

Tabby looked at George. He looked very grown up
and happy. "Yes, please," she replied.

Tabby lifted up her leaf saucer and pine-cone teacup,
and George poured the tea.

23

"Hey," said Tabby, "why don't we invite the others?"

"I don't know," George said, shrugging his shoulders.
"I don't want to clutter the place."

Gem nudged George and said, "As I was saying,
it's good to have some friends sometimes."

"We're your friends," Tabby said. Then she called down,

"Everyone, come up to George's tree-house!"

And everyone came up, one by one.

"What's this sack?" asked Fred.

"That's the tablecloth," said George. "Mind you don't get it dirty."

"What's this?" asked Leo, trying to untangle a bunch of sticks from his hair.

"That's the chandelier, can't you see?"

"We were just having tea," said Tabby.

George poured everyone a cup of tea from the teapot. Tabby was holding her leaf saucer in one hand and lifting her pine-cone teacup with the other. Everyone did the same.

"Would you like some cake?" George asked his friends.

"What kind have you got?" asked Fred, licking his lips.

"Chocolate," said George.

"Oh, that's my favourite," said Fred. "Don't mind if I do."

And he helped himself to a great big piece of bark.

Everyone had a marvellous time in George's tree-house.

"Thanks for having us," said George's friends,

after finishing the tea and cake.

"You always have the best ideas,"

George said to Gem as they were walking home.

"As I was saying," said Gem, "it's good to have some friends sometimes."

Top of the Class
Collect them all!

Ellie Takes a Chance
Zuza Vrbova
Illustrated by Tom Morgan-Jones
1-84458-483-6

Zoë Wins the Race
Zuza Vrbova
Illustrated by Tom Morgan-Jones
1-84458-407-0

Piers Finds his Voice
Zuza Vrbova
Illustrated by Tom Morgan-Jones
1-84458-406-2

George Makes Friends
Zuza Vrbova
Illustrated by Tom Morgan-Jones
1-84458-482-8

Tabby Saves the Day
Zuza Vrbova
Illustrated by Tom Morgan-Jones
1-84458-481-X

Kit Paints the Sky
Zuza Vrbova
Illustrated by Tom Morgan-Jones
1-84458-404-6

Leo Takes to the Stage
Zuza Vrbova
Illustrated by Tom Morgan-Jones
1-84458-405-4

Roddy Learns a Lesson
Zuza Vrbova
Illustrated by Tom Morgan-Jones
1-84458-480-1

Visit the Top of the Class website at
www.topoftheclassbooks.com